The Boy Who Walked on Water

and other stories

Written by
VIVIAN FRENCH

Illustrated by
CHRIS FISHER

WALKER BOOKS
AND SUBSIDIARIES
LONDON • BOSTON • SYDNEY

*For the children of the
Orkneys and the Western Isles –
with my love*

*Do chloinn nan
Eileanan Siar agus Arcaibh –
le gaol*

First published 1999 by Walker Books Ltd
87 Vauxhall Walk, London SE11 5HJ

This edition published 1999

2 4 6 8 10 9 7 5 3 1

Text © 1999 Vivian French
Illustrations © 1999 Chris Fisher

This book has been typeset in Plantin Light

Printed in England by Clays Ltd, St Ives plc

British Library Cataloguing in Publication Data
A catalogue record for this book is
available from the British Library.

ISBN 0-7445-6397-6

CONTENTS

He walked as easily on water as he did on the ground.

THE BOY WHO WALKED
ON WATER

Once there was a boy who could walk on water. He lived with his grandfather and his mother on an island where the sea crept into the land with long twisting fingers, and rivers and streams wound round and round and in and out until the island was a patch-work of rocks and hills and fields sewn together with strips of shining water.

Although the island was small it was not easy to travel from East to West, or North to South, for there were always saltwater lakes to walk around or rivers or streams to cross. The boy, Fergal, had no such problem. As soon as he could walk at all he walked as easily on water as he did on the ground. He walked on the streams and the lakes and the rivers, and even the sea. "Look at that," said his mother. "Now, there's a gift." His grandfather said nothing. He was a fisherman, as were all the islanders, and he had seen and thought many things while he was rocking in his boat on the northern seas. A grandson who could walk on water was certainly strange, but there was, most likely, a reason for it somewhere.

When Fergal was a little boy he did not notice that he was different from other children. After all, every winter, when cold winds came sweeping down from the North, the sea froze, and the lakes and rivers and streams of the island turned into solid blocks of clouded silver ice. All the children whooped and slithered and slid, and Fergal slid with them. Even when the spring came and the ice and snow melted away, Fergal played happily with his friends. Some of them were good at running races. Others were expert at walking on wooden stilts. Ailsa could swing herself round and round in cartwheels. Fergal could walk on water. If the older children looked at him strangely and whispered behind their hands, Fergal never noticed. The adults said nothing at all. They agreed with Fergal's grandfather. There was probably a reason somewhere, and if there wasn't, well, it did the boy no harm, nor anyone else as far as they could see.

As Fergal grew, things changed, and not for the better. He was a shy, quiet boy who wanted nothing more than to be like everyone else – but no one else could do what he did. Two or three children began to tease him, and soon, the others joined in.

"Fergal's a water beetle!" they called after him.

Their parents told them to leave Fergal alone. "He can't help the way he is," they said. "Don't bother him." But the children took no notice. They ran after Fergal and danced in circles round him.

"Fergal the frog!" "Maybe he's been bewitched!" "He's not like us!" "Fergal's STRANGE!"

Ailsa slipped her hand into his, and told him not to mind.

Fergal became quieter still, and more thoughtful. His mother noticed that he now hopped across the stream on the stepping-stones, and walked all the way down to the bridge to cross the river. When it was warm enough to splash and swim in the sea Fergal

Children began to tease him.

was nowhere to be seen.

"Where have you been?" Ailsa asked him.

"I had to help my mother in the house," Fergal told her, but his mother was sitting down on the harbour's edge mending nets.

As time went by the children slowly forgot that Fergal had once been able to walk on water. All they remembered was that he was in some way different, and however hard he tried he was never at the centre of the laughing groups of boys and girls. Only Ailsa called for him to join them as they ran races on the sand or jumped from rock to rock. Only Ailsa caught his hand and dragged him into games of tag or catch-me-as-you-can. If Ailsa was busy looking after her little brothers and sisters Fergal was left alone. He would go for long solitary walks North and South and East and West, but he never once walked on water.

"Be careful," his grandfather told him. "Gifts are given to be used, not to be hidden."

Fergal turned away.

The storm came early one morning as the last fishing boat sailed into the harbour. It was the most terrible storm that the islanders had ever lived through; far more wild than the storm that had drowned Fergal's father on the day that Fergal was born. Black clouds came swirling up and covered the island in darkness, and tearing winds wrenched bushes out of the earth and hurled them into the air. For three days and nights the sea roared and growled and clawed at the island until the shores and cliffs were raw and ragged. The fishermen's boats were snatched from the harbour and tossed into the howling tempest as if they were walnut shells, and the huge rocks and slabs of granite that made up the harbour wall were cracked and splintered until they lurched broken into the heaving waves around them.

When at last the storm was over the islanders walked silently down to the shore. They did not speak. There was nothing to say. There was no harbour, no protecting wall and not one boat. The younger children ran about picking up strips of seaweed and scraps of sailcloth that lay scattered on the sand and stones, but the older ones looked anxiously at their parents.

"Will we build the harbour again?" a boy asked his father.

His father shook his head. "What for?" he said, and his voice was bleak. "We have no boats to keep there."

"We can find wood and make more

14

boats," said a girl.

Her mother sighed. "You know there are no trees here. We trade our fish for wood … and without our boats there will be no fish."

"No fish, and nothing else besides," said an old man. "All our livelihood is gone. There's nothing left for us now."

"Look! Look!"

Ailsa's father had climbed out on the cliff above the tumbled heaps of stone where the harbour wall had stood. Now he was shouting and waving his arms. "A boat!" he shouted. "I can see a boat!" Other islanders rushed to join him, and Ailsa and Fergal scrambled after them. They shaded their eyes and stared over the sea, and wondered about the dark speck way out across the heaving and rolling waves.

"Whatever it is we must fetch it in!" said Ailsa's father. "If it's nothing but wreckage we can save the wood … and if it is a boat we can begin again! We can search for our fishing boats … we can fish … we can live!" And he tore off his heavy boots and coat and leapt down the cliff to plunge into the cold water.

"No! No!" Ailsa ran after her father, but she was too late. He was already striding deeper and deeper into the swell of the tide. An incoming wave knocked him off balance and Ailsa gasped as he sank beneath the steel grey water, but he came up spluttering. He was still looking ahead to the horizon. The islanders watched silently as he began to swim with short jerky strokes. None of them were strong or able swimmers. They believed, like most fishermen, that it was better to drown quickly than to swim on and on and die a slow and lingering death.

*   *   *

16

The islanders watched silently as he began to swim.

Ailsa's face was white. Even as her father stared steadily ahead of him so she watched her father. His black head, glistening like a seal, moved further and further away from the shore and safety.

Fergal looked at Ailsa, and then out across the rippling sea. Was it a boat? If it was, it was tossing and teasing at the edge of sight. Surely no one could swim so far. Fergal turned, and walked to the water's edge. As he stepped out from the sand there was a roar from the rocks above. "Murdo's in trouble! He's sinking! He can't go any further!"

No one saw Fergal take his first step. They were far too intent on shouting and calling to Ailsa's father to see that Fergal, for the first time in his life, was paddling – that he was not walking on water but splashing in the shallow lapping waves. Fergal stood still. His gift was gone.

"Fergal! FERGAL!" It was Ailsa, flying down the shore towards him. "Fergal – save him! Save my father!"

"Go, boy, go!" His grandfather was beside him. "Now's the time, Murdo's drowning! Help him, boy, help him! Walk on water!"

Fergal took another step, and the waves splashed against him so that he stumbled. He turned, his face white as Ailsa's, and held out his hands. "Ailsa!" he said. "It won't work for me any more!"

Ailsa stared at him, her eyes wide.

"You do it," said Fergal, and he touched her arm. "Walk on water, Ailsa – GO!"

And Ailsa was walking on the water. She was walking, she was running, she was skimming the surface like a seagull.

The islanders held their breath as she flew over the tossing waves, over the white foam.

She reached her father as he struggled to the surface for the third time, coughing and gasping, his lungs bursting with the desire for air. Ailsa reached down to him, and there were the two of them standing hand in hand on the water as if it were nothing more than a shifting sheet of glass under their feet. Together they turned to the horizon.

All the men and women and children standing on the cliff top stared. They rubbed their eyes and wondered if they had really seen what they thought they had seen. They shook their heads and told each other that the mist was coming up over the sea, and it was easy to see strange things in mist. They told the children not to be so foolish. How could they imagine that two people could walk together on water, hand in hand? But all the same, Ailsa and her father were gone.

Had they both drowned? Or would they come back? Could they come back?

"We'll watch and wait," said Fergal's grandfather, and it was agreed that this was all that could be done.

It was almost dark when Ailsa and her father came back to the island. The sun was sinking low into the West, and stars were creeping up the violet sky. The little boat came dancing over the waves with the evening wind behind it, its sail bellying out triumphantly. The islanders raised a cheer that shook the seabirds off the rocks, and hurried to haul the boat high up on the shingle. Ailsa and her father were carried shoulder high, up and away to where a fire was blazing on the headland to light them home. There was singing and dancing and feasting, and when Ailsa's father told how he and Ailsa had seen more of their boats beached on a bare island not too far to the North the cheering reached the moon itself.

"Murdo has saved us all!" a boy shouted.

"Aye! Aye! Three cheers for Murdo and Ailsa!"

"Murdo who swam to save us!"

"Murdo the seal swimmer!"

Ailsa's father Murdo nodded his head, but Ailsa jumped up.

"We didn't swim!" she said. "It was Fergal. Fergal gave me his gift! We walked on water!"

The islanders nodded and smiled at Ailsa, but they went on singing and celebrating. Soon it was understood that Murdo the seal swimmer had swum halfway across the ocean to save the island. And Ailsa? Some said Ailsa had swum after him … and

Ailsa slipped away from the flickering lights.

a few said she walked on water. Most islanders shook their heads. Hadn't they told the same story of Fergal ... and was that true? No!

Ailsa slipped away from the flickering lights of the fire. "Fergal!" she called into the darkness, "Fergal!"

There was no answer. Ailsa went down to the shore. Fergal was sitting on a stone, his feet in the water, listening to the waves as they whispered and sighed in and out of the little stones under his toes.

"Fergal!" said Ailsa, and she ran to him. "Fergal, I've lost your gift! When Father and I found the boat it left us. Will it come back to you?"

Fergal shook his head. "I don't think so," he said, and he looked down. "I don't want it. I've never known what water felt like before today. It feels like cold silk. It's so beautiful!"

Ailsa shivered. "Beautiful," she said, "but dangerous too."

Fergal picked up a pebble and tossed it into the water. It fell with a splash, and Ailsa laughed and threw another pebble after it. Then she caught at Fergal's hand, and pulled him to his feet. "Come on," she said. "I can hear the fiddler playing up on the cliff. Come and dance!"

"We can dance here," said Fergal, and he and Ailsa held hands and twirled and whirled round and round on the sandy shore. Neither of them noticed the pebbles as they bobbed back up to the surface of the sea as easily as if they were corks, and floated slowly away upon the outgoing tide.

Every day the potmender walked down to the village.

The Old Potmender
and the Tin Tea Kettle

Not so very long ago there was a potmender who lived with his wife in a tiny cottage tucked away in the side of a hill. Every day he walked down to the village below and went from house to house looking for work. The people of the village were not rich, and if their saucepans and frying pans and baking tins wore out they had no money to buy new ones. They waited for the pot-mender to call, and he would put a metal patch over the hole and solder it into place. Then they could use the pan again because it wouldn't leak any more – and if it did, it was only a little. They paid the potmender a few pennies for his help and he would walk home happily, jingling his money in his pocket.

The days and the weeks and the years went by and the potmender grew old. There didn't seem to be so many pots and pans to mend, and those that did need mending belonged to the poorest villagers who had hardly a penny to spare. As well as growing old the potmender grew hungry, and his wife grew angry. One evening he came home with nothing at all. He came slowly up the path to his house, opened the door and put down his bag of tools as quietly as he could. Looking nervously around he tiptoed inside, hung up his coat and crept towards his tattered old armchair.

"Potmender! Is that you at last?" His wife came screeching towards him, her hair on

end and a wooden spoon in her hand. Behind her the tin tea kettle bubbled and hissed on the fire.

"Yes, dear," said the potmender, and he sighed.

"And how much money have you made today?"

The potmender sighed again. "Nothing."

"And why not?" His wife banged the spoon on the table and the potmender jumped. "I suppose you've been mending pots and pans for free."

The potmender sighed for the third time. "They didn't have any money," he said. "But they did thank me very much."

"Did they indeed?" said his wife. "And since when did a thank you ever pay for bread and cheese?"

The potmender fished in his pocket. "Old Granny Green gave me two silver buttons."

"Buttons!" His wife leapt in the air in fury. "Buttons! How are we to eat? How are we to mend the roof? How are we going to pay the rent? Buttons, indeed!" And each time she said "Buttons!" she banged the table, and each time she came closer and closer to the potmender until she was waving the spoon right in front of his nose. The tin tea kettle hopped and fizzed on the fire and rattled its lid, but the potmender's wife took no notice. She glared at the potmender.

"You go straight out of that door," she said, "and don't come back until you've got a pocketful of money! Not buttons, mind – *money!*"

"Oh, wife," the potmender said wearily, "I'll try and do better tomorrow... I'm so tired now. Couldn't I just sit by the fire and have a little bread and cheese? And maybe a pickle or two, to help it down?"

"No!" shouted his wife, and she waved the spoon more wildly than ever. "There'll be no bread and cheese until you bring in some money! Not a crumb! Not a rind! Not the sniff of a pickle! *Be off with you!*"

The potmender went slowly to the door.

"I'm going," he said. "I'm going." He pulled his coat down and began to struggle into it, muttering as he did so. "I do wish she'd leave me alone. I try my best. I really do. I wish she'd go away somewhere, so I could have a little peace. But where could she go? Nowhere that's far enough away to give me a rest..." He shook his head as he picked up his bag of tools. "Nowhere ... maybe even that's too near. I wish she'd go away to ... to the other side of Nowhere!" He put out his hand to open the door, and then stopped.

*   *   *

31

It was very quiet. Amazingly quiet. The old potmender rubbed his eyes and looked round.

"Wife?" he said. "Wife? Where are you?"

There was no answer.

"Wife!" The potmender hunted round the bare little room. He opened an empty cupboard and peered under the table.

"*Wife!* Where are you? Please come back!"

There was no sound except for the bubbling of the kettle. The potmender sat down and gazed into the fire. "Wherever can she be? One minute she was here, and the next – *gone!* It's very odd, it is indeed."

"No it's not. *Sssssssss!*"

The potmender sat bolt upright. Whoever had spoken had a hissing, spitting voice. "Who's that?" he asked nervously. "And where are you?"

There was an even louder hiss. "*Sssssssss!*

Here I am!" And the tin tea kettle swung itself off the fire and winked at the potmender. "Aren't you going to thank me?"

The potmender couldn't say anything. He sat and stared. The tin tea kettle began to hiss and bubble and dance up and down.

"No more shouting? No more nagging? You can sit in front of the fire and toast your toes in peace and quiet ... for ever and ever and ever!"

The potmender went on staring. "I don't understand," he said. "What's happened? Where's my wife?"

"How stupid you are!" the tin tea kettle hissed. "You wished your wife would go away, didn't you? And so she has – I made your wish come true! She's blown away – blown away to the other side of nowhere! Oh, how clever, how clever, how clever I am!" And the tea kettle spun itself round in a circle and puffed steam all over the room.

"Oh!" said the potmender, and he jumped up. "Oh, my poor wife! What have I done? Where is she? Oh, dearie dearie me!" He hurried to the door. "I didn't mean it – whatever will she be thinking? Poor thing – she'll be so lonely all by herself on the other side of wherever it is – I must find her!" He opened the door and looked back at the tea kettle. "Please tell me where to go – where should I start?"

The tin tea kettle let out a long and piercing whistle of disgust. "*Sssssssssssssss!* So *this* is all the thanks I get! But you'll never find her. Never, never, never! Tee hee hee! You wanted her on the other side of Nowhere, and that's where she is … for ever and ever and ever!" And it blew one last hiss of steam and disappeared up the chimney with a hop and a skip.

"Sssssssssssssss! So this is all the thanks I get!"

The old potmender swung his toolbag on to his shoulder and shut the door behind him. He shivered as the cold wind sliced through his thin coat.

"If that tea kettle won't help me I'll go on my own," he said to himself. "The other side of Nowhere! Wherever can that be? I know, I'll go down to the village. Someone there is sure to be able to tell me. *Brrrr!* Perhaps I'll feel warmer if I walk a little faster." And he set off down the path as the first few drops of rain began to fall.

The night grew darker and darker, and the rain grew heavier. The old potmender began to slip and slide as he hurried along, and he wished that he had brought a lantern. Branches tugged at his coat, and twisted roots caught at his feet.

"The path to the village is never as hard as

36

this," the potmender muttered to himself as he struggled through a tangle of thorns. "I must have lost my way—" And as he spoke a gust of wind and rain rushed at him from behind and sent him rolling over and over into the darkness.

The potmender sat up and rubbed his head. It was so dark he could see nothing at all, but he was out of the wind and rain. Something heavy was lying on his feet; he put out a hand and found his toolbag. Carefully he felt all around. He seemed to be lying on something soft … leaves, he thought, and he yawned. "At least it's warm and dry in here," he said. "I might as well stay put until morning." He yawned again. "I'm so tired…" He pulled his toolbag under his head as a knobbly pillow, shut his eyes and went to sleep.

The old potmender woke up slowly. He was aching all over, and his head was sore. He opened his eyes, trying to remember where he was, and saw the sun shining in from a wide opening between tall grey rocks.

"I must have fallen into a cave," he said, and began to struggle to his feet. He was half-way up when he stopped, and sniffed. He could smell a wonderful warm sweet smell. He sniffed again. "Hot chocolate!" said the potmender, and he scrambled out of the cave.

Outside the sun was bright and the sky was blue.

"I'm sure I've never been here before," said the potmender, as he looked at the hill-side of grass and stones. "Wherever can I be? And – goodness gracious me! *Whatever* is that down there?"

Down below him a river ran splashing and gurgling between the rocks. A dark brown river; a river that steamed and bubbled and boiled … and smelt of cosy evenings by the fire with comforting mugs of hot cocoa.

The potmender scratched his head. "I do believe it's a hot chocolate river! It really is! It's very strange, very strange indeed. Maybe I'm going the right way to find my wife after all … when you think about it, the other side of Nowhere is sure to be different from our village." And the potmender nodded to himself and began climbing down towards the chocolate river, his bag of tools jangling on his back.

Halfway down he paused. Something was running along the riverbank. Or was it running? The potmender screwed up his eyes. No, it wasn't running. It was hopping, hopping on one leg and waving its arms like a windmill.

"Oh dear," said the potmender. "I do

hope it's not dangerous." He hesitated for a moment. "It isn't very big. And it might be able to tell me if I'm on the right road." He went on climbing over the rocks and stones.

By the time the potmender reached the river the smell of hot sweet chocolate was very strong indeed. It made his eyes water and his stomach rumble with hunger, but he was too busy gazing at the odd little figure in front of him to think about eating or drinking. It had stopped hopping and was crouched on a rock that leant right over the steaming river. The potmender edged a little closer.

"Why," he said to himself, "it's fishing up hot chocolate in a tiddly old saucepan! Maybe it'd let me have a sip or two?" He took a step nearer. As he did so the little creature pulled the saucepan out of the river and boiling chocolate splashed all over its small furry feet.

"*Oh! Oh! Oh!*" it shrieked, and began hopping and jumping just as it had done before. The potmender shrank back as it whirled its saucepan round and round. Gradually it began to calm down, but it went on whimpering and moaning. The potmender saw that its feet were covered in blisters and boils.

Poor little thing, he thought, and then he caught sight of the saucepan. "*Goodness!*" He was so surprised he spoke out loud. "That's the biggest hole I've ever seen!"

"What? What's that?" The creature pricked up its long ears. "What did you say?"

The potmender took the saucepan. "Just look at that hole!" he said. "You can't use it like that!"

"But I must! I'm the Drinker!"

The potmender shook his head. "You'll

41

not be doing much drinking out of a pan like that."

"No," said the Drinker, and its ears drooped. "I don't."

"I could mend this," the potmender said, and he turned the little pan over and over. "It's not worn through everywhere." He swung his bag off his shoulder and sat down. The Drinker squatted down beside him and looked hopefully at the tools the potmender was laying out on the grass.

"Can you really make it better?" it asked.

"I should think so," the potmender said. "I'll need a few sticks to make a fire, though."

The Drinker jumped up. "Easy!" It skipped off, and was back in no time carrying an armful of sticks and twigs and dry leaves.

"Grand!" The potmender built a small fire and lit it with his tinder-box. The

Drinker sat as close as it could and watched.

"What will you do?" it asked.

"Why, mend this hole, of course," said the potmender. "Then your pan will be as good as new."

The Drinker looked at the saucepan in surprise. "I thought it *was* new. I thought it was meant to be like that."

The potmender blew on his fire. The flames began to crackle and to burn, and he pulled out a piece of metal from his bag. "Here," he said. "I'll put this over the hole and solder it in place, and – *oh!*"

"What is it? What is it?" The Drinker stared at him.

"How could I have forgotten? I used my last little end of solder on Granny Green's frying pan."

The Drinker began to tremble. "Is that bad? Is it very bad?"

"Try it now," he said.

The potmender sighed, and pushed his hands into his pockets. "There's nothing I can do without a scrap of solder," he said sadly.

"Oooh," moaned the Drinker. "Ooooh."

"Wait!" The potmender shook his coat and something jingled. "Look here! The two silver buttons Granny gave me! I can use one of those..." And he set to work.

By the time the potmender had finished the sun was high in the sky. He wiped his forehead and handed the little saucepan to the Drinker.

"Try it now," he said.

The Drinker smiled an enormous smile and scurried to the river's edge. Carefully he bent down, and carefully he filled the pan.

"It's *full*!" he called out. "It hasn't spilled a drop! Oh, now I can drink and drink and drink!" And he lifted the panful of steaming chocolate and drank it in one gulp.

"That would burn my mouth for sure," the potmender said as he tidied up his tools.

The Drinker swung round. "Thank you, thank you!"

The potmender sighed, and picked up his bag. "I'd best be on my way," he said. "I shouldn't really have stopped so long. I'm looking for my wife. I don't suppose you'd know where the other side of Nowhere is?"

The Drinker put down his saucepan. "Try the other side of the river."

The potmender was so surprised that he dropped his bag.

"Oh yes," said the Drinker. "Over there on the other side of the river is Somewhere, and in Somewhere you'll find the Somebodies. They know about *everything*, so they're sure to be able to tell you where Nowhere is.

46

And then – pip! – you just have to find the other side of it." The Drinker leant down and filled his saucepan again. "Have a little drink before you go."

"Thank you kindly." The potmender took the saucepan gratefully and blew on the chocolate to cool it. As he sipped he looked up and down the bubbling river. "That's splendid news, that is. The Somebodies, you say? Just splendid. Where's the bridge?"

"Bridge? There's no bridge."

The potmender choked on his last mouthful. "But how will I get across?"

There was a silence. The Drinker opened and shut his mouth several times, and pulled at his whiskers. "I don't know," he said at last.

"Is there a boat?" The potmender looked anxious. "I *must* get across to the other side and find those Somebody folk. My wife's sure to be wondering why I'm not there to fetch her home."

"No boat." The Drinker drooped over his furry feet.

The potmender sat down and held his head. "Oh, dearie dearie dearie."

"*Eeeek!*" The Drinker leapt into the air. "I know! I know! The Freezer! He'll *freeze* the river, and then you can slide across on the chocolate ice!"

The potmender looked up at the wildly spinning Drinker.

"What's that?"

"The Freezer! Quick! Call him now!"

"And he'll get me across the river?"

"Yes! Yes! He'll freeze it!" The Drinker sprang at the potmender and pulled him to his feet. "Now! Call his name! As loudly as you can!"

The potmender cupped his hands round

his mouth. "Mr Freezer!"

"Louder!" said the Drinker. *"Louder!"* And he hopped a little way up the hill.

The potmender tried again. *"Mr Freezer! Mr Freezer!"*

"Louder!" The Drinker was moving further and further away. "Louder! Louder..." And his own voice faded.

The potmender took a deep breath. "MR FREEZER! MR FREEZER! Oh, please come! PLEASE COME, MR FREEZER!"

A chilly breeze sprang up from nowhere. A grey cloud swept across the sun and was swiftly followed by others, each darker than the one before. A flurry of snowflakes swirled round the old potmender's head, and an icy wind cut through his thin coat and made him shiver. The snow hissed and spat as it drove down the hill and into the river, and clouds of steam billowed up into the darkening sky. The potmender shuddered and pulled his coat tightly round him.

"WHO ARE YOU THAT DARES TO CALL ME FROM MY HOME AMONG THE SNOWS AND STORMS?"

The potmender turned slowly, his teeth chattering. An enormous figure was staring down at him with glittering frosty eyes.

"Excuse me, my Lord," the potmender said, his voice shaking, "but I need to cross the river..."

"AND WHAT CONCERN IS THAT OF MINE?"

The potmender shook his head. "None, sir. I see that now, and I'm ever so sorry to have bothered you. I just thought..."

"THOUGHT? WHAT DID YOU THINK?"

"That you could ... that you could freeze the river. Well, that is, if it's not too much trouble..."

The Freezer swung round, the pale folds of his cloak whirling about him. The potmender sank to his knees, his arms over his head.

"BUT IT IS A TROUBLE! WHAT WILL YOU GIVE ME FOR MY TROUBLE?"

"I have very little," the potmender whispered. "All I have are my tools. You can have my tools... Or a silver button..."

"WHAT USE ARE THOSE TO ME?" The Freezer flicked his long blue fingers, and a hailstorm burst into the frozen air. The potmender crouched lower as the hailstones rattled about him.

"I HAVE NO NEED OF SUCH THINGS. NO ... YOU MUST GIVE ME YOUR COAT!" And the Freezer laughed.

The Freezer's laugh chilled the potmender as he had never been chilled before. He nodded, unable to speak, and slowly, for his

A hailstorm burst into the frozen air.

hands were numb with cold, pulled off his skinny old coat.

"MY THANKS, POTMENDER!" The Freezer tossed the coat on to his back, and the potmender saw that the Freezer's cloak was entirely made of scarves and coats and cloaks and jackets and shawls, all of them worn to threads and heaped one upon another. "AND NOW – BE GONE!"

There was such a stinging slap of snow on the potmender's face that he shut his eyes. He felt himself sliding, and could not stop. He was so cold that he could not think; where was he? What was he doing? As snowflakes and hailstones drove against him he fought his way onwards, staggering at each step. He came to a heap of rocks and began slowly to crawl over them. The wind shrieked and wailed, and needles of icy sleet beat down on him. The old potmender sank to the ground. The cold crept up and over him, and he slipped into a frozen sleep.

Above the potmender the winds raged and howled a while longer. Then there was a whistle, a clear cold whistle from the frozen North. Swirling round in a circle, the winds raced away, and the clouds drifted apart. The sun came out and warmed the earth and the snow began to melt.

"Potmender! Potmender!"

The potmender rubbed his eyes and sat up. Had he really heard something? It was the very faintest of cries, and far, far away.

"Potmender! Potmender!" It was fainter still, a thin thread of sound.

"Wife!" The potmender struggled to his feet. "Where are you? I'm coming!" And he began to hurry along the path as fast as he could go. He puffed as he scrambled round

boulders and through long tangled grass, and it was only when he stopped to catch his breath that he noticed the snow had gone.

The potmender looked around him in amazement. "There's no sign of all that snow! And it's quite warm!" He climbed up a small bank and looked around. "Well, I never! There's the hot chocolate river – and it's behind me! I must have crossed it in all that snow, and I never knew." He sat down and wiped his forehead. "So here I am on the other side. Why, this must be Somewhere! I must hurry along and find those Somebodies … whoever they might be." And he set off along the winding track in front of him.

Gradually the track became a path, and the path became a road. It was a fine road, an important-looking road, and it made the potmender feel that he shouldn't really be walking along it. The road was so wide and smooth and clean, and he was so dusty and dirty. Every so often it gave a little twitch and a sniff, and when the potmender took to trotting along in the ditch the road gave a loud sigh of relief.

I wonder where I should look for these Somebodies, the potmender thought. I expect they live somewhere really grand. A road like this must be going somewhere very wonderful. He pulled his belt a little tighter and sighed. "I just hope they have something there for me to eat."

"Good morning, dear sir!"

"Why, dear sir, good morning to you!"

The potmender looked up from his ditch. A hugely round person was rolling slowly down the road. Another hugely round person was rolling in the other direction, and they met with a gentle bump. They took no notice of the potmender.

"A fine day!"

"A very fine day!"

"A very, very, very fine day!" And they bowed and nodded and smiled at each other.

"Excuse me!" The potmender scrambled out of his ditch. The road shuddered, but the two hugely round people went on bobbing and beaming exactly as if he had never spoken.

"Excuse me," the potmender said again, "but would you please very kindly tell me if you are the Somebodies?"

The first round person quivered. "Did you hear something, dear sir?"

"Why, dear sir, I think that I did."

"Should we answer, dear sir?"

The second round person gave the potmender the speediest of glances.

"No, dear sir. I think we need not." And it smiled a fat wide smile and bowed and nodded and bowed again.

The potmender shook his head. Then he pinched himself and rattled his bag of tools. "It seems to me that I'm as real as ever I was," he said to himself, "so how come they don't seem to see me?" He took a step forward and cleared his throat.

"Ahem. Excuse me, but I'm looking for the Somebodies. Is it you, or isn't it?"

The road gave a horrified wriggle, but the two hugely round people merely raised their eyebrows at each other.

"Did it speak again, dear sir?"

"You know, dear sir, I think that it did."

"Did it address us by name, dear sir?"

"Dear sir, dear sir, I fear that it didn't." The second round person rolled even closer to the first, and whispered in a loud and carrying whisper, "It would seem, dear sir, *that it doesn't know who we are!*" And both of them flapped their hands in horror and rolled their eyes.

"Such ignorance, dear sir!"

"Indeed, dear sir. Should we tell him?"

"It would, dear sir, be only kind."

And the two hugely round people rolled themselves in a circle so that they were facing the potmender. They bowed to each other once more, and then spoke.

"Know, you small and dusty thing—"

"that *we*, you unimportant nothing—"

"*are indeed...*" they paused and bowed deeply, "...THE SOMEBODIES!"

The potmender stared. The two Somebodies were beaming their fat wide smiles at each other, and patting each other warmly on the back.

"Well said, dear sir!"

"Dear sir, well said!"

"Just a moment!" The potmender went on staring. "Just a moment! You say *you* are the Somebodies?"

The two Somebodies chuckled fatly.

"We are indeed!"

"Indeed we are!"

The potmender put down his bag of tools. All sorts of thoughts were tumbling through his head.

"Somebodies?" he said. "You call yourself *Somebodies?* When you couldn't even be bothered to give me a good morning or a how d'you do? Let me tell you, that's not being a Somebody. Where I come from a Somebody is someone who is kind, and helpful, and who has time for you. Somebody who'll ask you if you're lost, and show

you the way. Somebody who'll help you find your poor lost wife who's somewhere in the middle of the other side of Nowhere and likely to stay there for ever and ever if all folk round here are like you. You're not Somebodies, you two. You're not anything at all! You're just puffed up with your own importance. You're – you're *Nobodies!*"

WHOOOOOOOOOOOOOOOOOOOOOSH!

The rush of air knocked the potmender head over heels, and the road trembled underneath him. He rolled over and over into his friendly ditch, and as he climbed out again his eyes widened. The Somebodies were shrivelling and shrinking, and as they shrank they squeaked and squawked and finally burst into tears.

"*Whooooooooooooooooooooo!*" they sobbed.

"*Whooooooooooo! Oooooooo! Ooooooooooo…*"

The potmender stared. The Somebodies looked like nothing so much as two crumpled heaps of clothes sitting on the edge of the road.

"*Oooooh!* Whatever shall we do?" they whimpered. "We're not Somebodies any more. We're nothing. Why, we must be – we must be – *Nobodies!*" And they began to wail louder than ever.

The potmender took a step towards them, not quite sure what to do. They looked so different he could hardly believe they had been the pompous and self-important Somebodies only a moment before.

"There, there," he said. "It's not that bad, being a Nobody. I'm a Nobody, and my wife's a Nobody, and we get on very well with it."

The Nobodies crept towards him.

"Whoooooooooooooooooooooo!" they sobbed.

"We're so sorry we were rude," whispered one.

"Dear sir, do forgive us!" whispered the other.

The potmender shrugged. "Don't you worry," he said. "We all make mistakes... But just don't do it again, that's all. And now if you'd be kind enough to tell me where I can find the other side of Nowhere, I'd be most grateful. I must be off to find my wife."

Instead of answering the two Nobodies began to sob loudly. "Nowhere!" they cried, "Nowhere! Oh, if we're Nobodies now we can't be living in Somewhere any more. Oh dear, oh dear, oh dear, we must be living in Nowhere!"

"Is that right?" The potmender picked up his bag and began to smile. "You mean I'm in Nowhere already? That *is* good news. Can you tell me where the other side is?"

There was no answer. The two Nobodies were sniffing, snuffling and blowing their noses.

"If we're Nobodies," one of them said slowly, "can we do *nothing?*"

The other one gave a little squeak. "Oh *yes!* Nothing to do!"

"Nothing all day!"

"Nothing *every* day!"

And they began patting each other on the back and bowing and bobbing and smiling.

The potmender sighed and left them to it.

"At least I'm doing well so far," he said, as he trudged away. "I'm sure to come to the other side sooner or later." He took a deep breath. "Wife! *Wife!* I DON'T KNOW IF YOU CAN HEAR ME BUT I'M ON MY WAY!"

"Tee hee hee! *Sssssssssssssssss!* Tee hee hee!

That's what *you* think!"

The potmender stopped dead. There, hissing and hopping on the path in front of him, was the tin tea kettle.

"Oh no!" said the potmender. "Not you again!" He frowned fiercely. "I'm on my way. I'll soon have my wife back, whatever you may think."

"Tee hee hee!" The tea kettle spun round and round and steam puffed out behind him. "It's a joke, it's a joke, don't you see what a joke it is? Tee hee hee!"

The potmender gripped his bag of tools tightly and went on walking. He was sure he was on the right road, and a tin tea kettle wasn't going to stop him now.

"*Sssssssssssssssss!*" The tea kettle danced in front of him blowing smoke rings. "You're so *stupid*! Don't you see? Your wife blew away to the other side of Nowhere … and the other side of Nowhere is Somewhere. You found yourself in Somewhere and what did you do? You turned it into Nowhere … you're going in circles, in circles, in circles!" And the tin tea kettle began to bubble and to boil madly as it cackled and snorted with glee.

The potmender stood quite still. He could hardly believe what the tin tea kettle was saying. He had come so far, and now it seemed he had only been walking in circles.

"You mean, you mean I was in the right place where I was before?" he asked. "Oh, my poor wife. Oh, what a bother this all is…" And he sat down wearily on the edge of the road.

"Tee hee! What a joke what a joke what a … *sssssssss*…" The tin tea kettle staggered. "*Sssssssss*…" it hissed, and it was no longer laughing. "*Sssssss* ... help! Help!" It sat down with a faint hiss at the potmender's feet. "Help me, potmender," it fizzled. "I think ... I've ... burst my sides ... help me..." And a thin trickle of water spread slowly into the ground.

The potmender folded his arms. "That serves you right," he said. "It really does. You're a nasty, wicked tea kettle and I don't see why I should help you after all you've done."

The tea kettle dribbled a little more. "If ... you don't help me ..." it hissed, "you'll ... never see your ... wife ... again."

The potmender stroked his chin thoughtfully. It certainly looked as if the tea kettle couldn't move. He came a little closer, and walked round it, keeping a safe distance in case this was another of its tricks.

"Hmm," he said, "you've split your side. There's quite a gap there."

"If … you … mend me … I'll … make … sure … you … and your wife … are together … for ever…"

"That's all very well," said the potmender. "But how do I know you're not playing another of your silly tricks?"

The tin tea kettle moaned a little. "I'll … show you."

The potmender watched suspiciously as the kettle began to rock itself to and fro. It murmured and it muttered in its thin weak voice and the faintest sizzling came from deep inside it. A tiny puff of steam floated into the air, and inside a small picture grew. Dimly the potmender could see his wife floating round and round in a never-ending circle of mist and smoke. She was calling out and, even though he couldn't hear her, the

69

potmender knew she was calling for him.

"I'm coming to find you, wife!" he shouted, but the picture faded away.

"Right!" The potmender began hurrying to and fro collecting dry sticks. He made up his fire, and opened his bag.

"Help!" whimpered the tin tea kettle. "Mend … me…"

"And what do you think I'm doing?" the potmender asked. He blew on the sticks and the flames burned high. He hunted in his bag for a piece of mending metal and felt for the silver button in his pocket.

"Dearie me," he said, and he sighed. "Fancy wasting a fine silver button on a wicked old tin tea kettle."

"*Sssssssssssss,*" said the tea kettle weakly. "*Sssssssssss…*"

The potmender began to heat his solder-

The potmender could see his wife floating

round and round.

ing iron. "Here we go. Although if it weren't for wanting my wife back I'd never be mending you at all." And he set to work patching up the tea kettle's side.

As the potmender finished, he blew out the fire. "There," he said. "You're not as good as new, but you'll do."

The tin tea kettle got up slowly. *"Sssssssss,"* it whispered. *"Sssssssss!"*

The potmender buckled up his bag of tools. "And now you'll send me and my wife home, if you please."

"Sssssssssssssssss!" hissed the tea kettle, and it began to spin. "Tee hee! Tee hee! Tee heeeeeee!" And as it spun it began to bubble and boil. "Here we go! *Sssssssss!* Here we go!" The potmender found himself spinning behind the kettle, faster and faster and faster.

"Hey!" he shouted, "What's going on? Where's my wife?"

"Here she issssssssssss!" the tea kettle fizzled and spat. "Here she issssss!" And as the potmender spun he saw his wife spinning beside him, round and round and round.

"Wife!" he called. "Wife!" He held out his hand, but she was spinning much too fast to catch it.

"*Ssssssssssssssssssssssssssssssssss!* Tee heeeee! Here you are! Together again! Together for ever! What a joke, what a joke, what a joke!" And the potmender saw the tea kettle hop and skip out of the circle that was spinning him and his wife up and down and round and round. The kettle slid away, and as it went the potmender could see puffs of steam shooting up into the air around it. Its lid was rattling with laughter, and it danced and sizzled with excitement.

"Together for ever! Spinning for ever! Round and round and—"

BAANNNNNGGGGGGGGG!

The explosion was so loud that the pot-mender clutched his ears as he fell in a heap on the ground. At the other side of the circle his wife screamed. Little pieces of tin flew into the air all around them, and clouds of steam gushed up. For a moment the pot-mender could see nothing at all, and then a figure came walking towards him through the steam.

"WIFE!"

"Oh, potmender! Is it really you at last?"

And the potmender and his wife held hands and smiled and smiled.

*   *   *

"Well, well, well," said the potmender. "Whoever would have believed such goings on! But now it's time to be getting back home … whichever way that might be!"

His wife glanced around. "I do believe we're on the path below our cottage!" She looked a little sideways at the potmender, and she blushed. "Potmender, dear," she said, "how would you like some supper? You must be ever so tired and hungry after such a terrible time as you've had." She let go of the potmender's hand, and twisted her apron. "I was thinking, up there in that circle. I was thinking, maybe I've been a little hard on you of late."

"Were you, wife?" asked the potmender, and he took her hand again as they walked towards their cottage.

"Yes," said his wife. "You do your best. I know that … and I have been shouting a little

75

too much. Just now and then."

The potmender opened his mouth in surprise, and then closed it firmly. "It's been a hard time for both of us, wife," was all he said.

"So we'll go home, shall we?" said his wife. "There's some bread and cheese in the cupboard."

"That would be fine," said the potmender. "And maybe a pickle or two?"

"And a pickle or two," his wife agreed.

And as they walked into their tiny cottage the potmender thought he could hear the merest whisper of a hiss and a chuckle...

"Oh, potmender! Is it really you at last?"

Behind the little grey town was a small hill.

WHY THE SEA IS SALT

Long ago there was a wide and rolling sea that lipped and lapped at the toes of a little grey town. The sea was as blue and green as a kingfisher's wing, and if you dipped and dabbled a hand in its sparkling waters, you would find that the drops on your fingers tasted as sweet as the water from a mountain stream.

Behind the little grey town was a small hill, and on the small hill was a little house. On the other side of the valley was a high hill, and on the high hill was a tall house. In the tall house lived a tall lean man. He was very rich, with a cellar full of gold and silver and kitchens full of puddings and pies and peaches and cream. In the little house lived a tiny woman with her seventeen children. They had no money at all, and their kitchen was quite empty – except for a pile of empty plates and a cobweb in the corner.

"What are we going to have for Christmas?" the children asked their mother one day. "Are we going to have presents? A tree? A turkey?"

The tiny woman shook her head.

"There's nothing to be had, my lovelies. I've nothing in my purse but a hole."

"Can't we ask our fine uncle up on the high hill to help us?" asked the eldest daughter. "He's got more than enough for all of us – and some more to spare besides."

"Oh no, Matilda," said the tiny woman. "My brother was mean as a boy, and he's mean as a man. He'll not give us a crumb for Christmas."

"But there's no harm in asking," said Matilda, putting on her shawl. "We won't be any worse off if he says no – and if he says yes, then we'll have a merry Christmas."

Matilda ran down the small hill, and trudged up the high hill.

The knocker on the door of the tall house was huge and heavy, and when Matilda lifted it and let it drop again the sound echoed and clanged all around her. The door opened slowly and heavily.

"Who is it?" asked Matilda's uncle in a deep dark voice.

"It's me, Uncle," said Matilda. "Christmas is coming, and we've nothing at all in the house except a pile of empty plates and a cobweb in the corner of the kitchen, so I thought that you might help us."

"Why?" asked the uncle.

Matilda scratched her head. "Well, perhaps because you're so kind?"

"I'm not," said the uncle.

"Ah," said Matilda. "Might you feel sorry for us?"

"No," said the uncle.

"But you are our uncle," said Matilda.

The uncle stepped forward.

"Did I ever ask your mother to have seventeen children?"

"Well, no, I don't suppose you ever did," Matilda said.

"And did I ever ask you to waste all your money on eating and drinking?"

"We did need to eat," said Matilda, "but you certainly didn't ask us to."

"And did I ever ask to be your uncle?"

"Well – no, I don't suppose you ever asked that either," Matilda said.

"Then," said the uncle, "I don't see why I should give you so much as a crumb for Christmas."

"That's what my mother said you'd say," said Matilda, turning to go. "But I said that there's no harm in asking. I'll wish you a happy Christmas and hurry off home."

"Just a minute!" The uncle turned and stamped away into his house.

Matilda waited on the doorstep.

What has he gone to get? she wondered. Biscuits? Ice-cream? Peppermints? Plums?

"Here you are." Her uncle was back, holding a plain green bottle and a brown paper parcel. "And don't you ever come bothering me again."

Matilda took the bottle and the parcel.

"Thank you very much, dear Uncle," she said. "Wouldn't you like to eat Christmas dinner with us?"

"I would not," said the uncle, and slammed the door shut.

Matilda began to run down the hill. Then she walked. Then she stopped.

"I wonder what's in the bottle?" she said to herself. "And what's in the parcel?"

Very carefully she opened the bottle. Very carefully she sniffed it. Then, very carefully, she tasted it.

"Oh," Matilda said. "Water." She sighed.

Very slowly she undid the string around the parcel. Very slowly she unwrapped the paper.

"Ugh," Matilda said. "Dried bacon."

"Ahem!"

"What?" Matilda jumped round.

A rusty dusty old man stood just behind her.

"Begging your pardon, my dearie, but

84

"Begging your pardon, my dearie…"

might I ask you for a bite to eat and a drop to drink?"

"There's never any harm in asking," said Matilda, "and you're more than welcome – but it's only water and some cold dried bacon."

The old man took a drink and a slice of meat. He chewed carefully and for a long time, and then he nodded his head.

"Thank you kindly, my dear, my deario. Now, have you a fine feast for Christmas?"

"Not exactly," Matilda said. "Only the bacon."

"Then listen to me. Do you have a long memory?"

"Yes, I do. I'm very good at remembering things," Matilda said.

"Good, that's good, my deario. Now, take your meat and water, and go through the woods to the darkest door. Knock three times and, whatever is offered to you, say, 'I want the churn behind the door.' Take nothing else."

"'I want the churn behind the door,'" Matilda repeated.

"Then you must hurry home – and remember one more thing – hip hop, little churn, hip hop stop!"

"I'll remember," said Matilda. "But what's a churn?"

"One, two, three – just wait and see!" There was a puff of wind, and Matilda sneezed. When she looked up, the little old man was nowhere to be seen. Matilda ran down the high hill and into the woods. In and out of the trees she hurried, looking about her. "Where's the darkest door?" she asked herself. "Where should I look?"

The trees were growing taller and darker. There was a rustling and a stirring as the wind began to blow.

"Ooooooh!" Matilda shivered.

A gust of wind blew a branch aside, and Matilda saw a door. It was the darkest door she had ever seen. Matilda shivered again.

"I want the churn behind the door," she said to herself. "Well, there's no harm in asking."

Matilda knocked once.

Nothing happened.

Matilda knocked again, louder.

No one answered.

She knocked again, as loudly as she could.

The door burst open with a crash that shook the ground under Matilda's feet. A dark, dark shadow swirled out through the doorway and glared at Matilda with red and staring eyes. Then it sniffed, and it snorted, and it sniffed again.

"Meat," it growled, "and water? *Give*

them to me!"

Matilda held on tightly to the green bottle and the brown paper parcel. She shook her head.

"I'll give you gold! Mountains of gold!" shouted the shadow.

Matilda tried to speak, but her voice seemed to have dried up into a little squeak.

"I want the churn behind the door," she whispered.

"MOUNTAINS AND RIVERS OF RUBIES AND GOLD!"

Black smuts of soot blew into Matilda's face. She coughed, and stamped her foot.

"I want the churn behind the door!"

There was a rush of wind, and the shadow towered above her holding something that looked like a barrel. Throwing it on the ground in front of Matilda, it snatched the green bottle and the piece of dried bacon from her hands.

The meat sizzled and scorched black, and the water bubbled and boiled and blew out a cloud of steam. The door shut with an echoing clang.

Matilda rubbed her eyes and looked about her. She was standing alone among the trees. There was a faint smell of burning in the air, but she could see no sign of a door at all.

She looked at the wooden barrel.

"So this is a churn," she said. "It looks very ordinary – just like a little barrel on legs, with a handle. I don't see what's so special about it."

Matilda picked up the churn and began to carry it back home. It was very heavy and awkward in her arms, and at the bottom of the small hill she sat down with a flump.

"I wish I'd kept the meat and water," she said crossly. "This churn is too heavy. I wish

I had something to drink."

The churn began to tremble and shake. Matilda's eyes grew wide as the handle slowly turned all by itself – chinkelly chunk, chunkelly chink. The top of the churn flew open and water began to pour out in a silvery stream.

Matilda tried to catch it in her hands, but it splashed between her fingers.

"Oh! Oh! Oh!" she said.

The churn went on turning. Chinkelly chunk, chunkelly chink it went. Matilda's feet were getting wet, and a shining lake was widening over the grass.

"Stop! Stop!" Matilda called. "That's plenty! Please stop!"

The churn went on churning.

"I thought you had a long memory," said a rusty voice in Matilda's ear.

"Of course!" she cried, clapping her

CHINKELLY CHUNK, CHUNKELLY CHINK.

hands. "I remember!" She leant towards the little churn. "Hip hop, little churn, hip hop stop!"

The churn stopped. Matilda began to laugh. All the water was sinking into the ground and she still had nothing to drink.

"I think I'd better go home," she said.

Matilda's mother and her brothers and sisters were waiting at the door of the house. When they saw Matilda coming they waved and shouted, and came running out to help.

"What is it? What is it? What is it?" they all asked at once.

"It's our Christmas dinner," Matilda said. "Just watch." She patted the churn. "Please may we have a Christmas dinner?"

CHINKELLY CHUNK, CHUNKELLY CHINK. Out of the churn came a table-cloth, flapping and floating through the air.

It settled on the table and was followed by knives and forks and spoons and cups and plates.

Then came all the most wonderful things to eat that Matilda and her brothers and sisters had ever dreamt of – and a great many things they had never thought of at all. Last of all came a pudding – a steaming plum pudding with a blue flame flickering over it and a sprig of holly on the top.

"Oooooh!" said all the children. Matilda smiled happily. "Hip hop, little churn, hip hop stop!" she whispered.

From that day on Matilda and her family were very happy. Whenever they needed anything they asked the churn, and the handle turned round and round until they had enough. They had five red hens, six fat sheep, seven plump pigs and eight black and white cows.

*　　*　　*

Up on the high hill the uncle watched and wondered.

"They said they had nothing but a pile of plates and a cobweb in the corner," he said to himself. "Where have these hens and sheep and pigs and cows come from?"

He pulled on his big black hat, swung his black cloak round his shoulders and set off down the high hill and up the small hill. When he reached the little house, he strode in through the front door without so much as a knock, and Matilda's tiny mother and all the children jumped up in surprise.

"Why, fancy seeing you, Brother!" said the mother. "Sit down, do, and let us tell you all about our good fortune." She patted the churn.

"Dear churn, give us a fine tea."

The uncle's eyes grew bigger and bigger as

the handle slowly began to turn. His mouth fell open as tea and cake and toast and jam floated out, up into the air and on to the table. He was so busy staring that he didn't notice at all when Matilda crept close to the churn and whispered, "Hip hop, little churn, hip hop stop."

"Our clever Matilda found it for us last Christmas," said the tiny woman. "She bargained for it with a piece of old dry bacon and a bottle of water."

"What?" roared the uncle, leaping to his feet.

Matilda's mother nodded. "Indeed she did, and what a fine thing it was for us all."

The uncle folded his arms.

"Just tell me," he growled, "who it was that gave Matilda that piece of meat?"

"Why, Brother – it was you!"

The tiny woman patted his arm.

"And who," the uncle asked, "gave Matilda that bottle of water?"

The tiny woman smiled happily.

"Why, Brother – you again! And very kind of you it was."

"Then," said the uncle with a greedy grin, "that churn is rightfully *mine!*"

He snatched up the churn, tucked it under his arm and marched out of the house. The tiny woman burst into tears.

"Don't cry, Mother," Matilda said. "Let's just wait for a little while, and see what happens." And she went to sit on the step outside the house.

The uncle carried the churn down the small hill. As he went striding up the high hill it grew heavier and heavier, and when the uncle reached his hallway he put it down with a grunt.

"Humph," he said. "Now, what shall I

start with? I know! Something to eat. And then I shall set you to work, little churn – churning gold until my cellars are full and running over. Maybe I shall build another barn to house my gold, and then another, and another, but now I'll have porridge!"

The uncle slapped the churn. "*Porridge!* Oh, and while you're at it, I'll have a couple of fine fresh fish – and hurry up about it."

The churn's handle began to jerk and twitch. Then – chinkelly chunk, chunkelly chink – it turned round and round, faster and faster. Porridge came pouring out in a thick stream, and fish popped out and flapped on to the ground in twos and threes, tens and twenties, forties and fifties.

"Stop!" roared the uncle. "That's enough!"

But the churn did not stop. On and on it

churned, and the porridge sucked and squelched about the uncle's feet, then his ankles, then his knees. Fish were heaped in piles all about him until the hallway was so full that they spilt out of the door and down the path.

The uncle shouted and growled and stamped and ranted, but it did no good. On and on went the churn – chinkelly chinkelly chunk, chunkelly chunkelly chink. At last the uncle began to wade down the hill, pushing heavily through the rising tide of porridge and fish.

"Help!" bellowed the uncle. *"Help!"* Matilda looked up from her seat on the step. She saw her uncle coming, and smiled a small secret smile.

"HELP!" Her uncle was red in the face and puffing and panting as he hurried towards Matilda. "HELP!"

"I'm being drowned in porridge and fish," he gasped.

"What is it, Uncle?" Matilda asked, getting up.

"I'm being drowned in porridge and fish," he gasped. "You must stop that churn – and then I'll chop it up for firewood!"

"Oh," said Matilda. She sat down again.

"What are you doing? You must come *now*, this very minute!" the uncle shouted very angrily.

"Well, I think I'd like to have my little churn back," Matilda said. " So if I stop the porridge, may I bring the churn home?"

"ANYTHING! JUST HURRY!" The uncle was turning from red to purple.

Matilda skipped down the small hill. As she climbed up the high hill, she saw that her uncle's house was slowly disappearing in a lake of porridge.

Matilda reached the hallway and seized the churn.

101

"Hip hop, my clever little churn," she said, "hip hop stop."

The churn stopped, and Matilda held it tightly as she slid and slithered back down the hill to her home. The uncle, staggering back up the high hill once more, shook his fist at the churn.

"My beautiful house! My cellars of gold! My puddings and pies and peaches and cream!" he wailed as he looked in his front door. "Ruined! All ruined!"

Matilda and her family had a celebration supper. Then they went on living very happily, apart from the days when the sun shone very strongly and the wind blew from the east. On those days there was a faint but unmistakeable smell of fish, and Matilda's tiny mother sent the children round the house to close all the windows.

"Perhaps we should move?" suggested Matilda.

"Perhaps we should," said her tiny mother, and the sixteen other children clapped their hands.

"Couldn't we live by the sea?" asked the littlest child.

Matilda and her mother and all the sixteen children moved into a tall white house on the edge of the harbour, and every day they watched the sparkling waters of the sea lapping at the toes of the little grey town. They watched the tall ships coming in and out, and loading and unloading their goods, and they were very happy. Matilda liked to sit on a pile of rocks at the harbour's entrance, and dabble her finger in the clean, clear water.

She was sitting there one day when a fine

white ship came cutting through the waves and tied up just beside her. A tall lean man in a black hat and a black cloak came hurrying down the gangplank, holding a large white handkerchief to his eyes and weeping and wailing and crying and sobbing.

"What is it?" Matilda asked. "Can I help you?"

"Dear child," said the man from behind his handkerchief. "Have pity on a poor sailor with nothing in the world but sixteen sad sisters and a pile of empty plates and a cobweb in the corner of the kitchen."

"Oh dear!" said Matilda, "I'm so very sorry – I know just how you feel. Oh!" she jumped up. "Wait here!"

Matilda hurried along the harbour wall and into her house. She found the churn and carried it back to where the poor sailor was snuffling into his handkerchief.

"Here," Matilda said. "Somebody gave this to me when I had nothing, and now I have everything I could want for. Please take it. It will bring you good fortune, too."

Matilda stopped. The sailor wasn't listening to her. He was hurrying away, back towards the fine ship, and as Matilda watched, he jumped on board and began hauling up the anchor. The sails filled in the breeze, and the ship swept away over the wide and rolling sea.

"Dear me," said Matilda. "And I never told him how my little churn works." She walked slowly back to her house.

On board the ship, Matilda's uncle was rubbing his hands together.

"This time," he gloated, "this time I shall make sure that I fill my houses and cellars and barns with gold – yes, and with rubies too. This time the churn will make me the richest man in all the world. I shall set it churning, churning, churning, and no matter to me if it never stops again. Indeed, if it churns for ever and ever so much the better."

Carrying the churn, the uncle went down into a magnificent cabin, hung about with red and silver. The captain met him in the doorway.

"So, where's your treasure?" he asked, staring at the little wooden churn. "What? What? What? All the promises you made to me, all the gold you said you'd give to me – all for an old barrel?"

The uncle smiled a sly, greedy smile.

"Just wait until your fine tall ship brings me to shore again," he said. "Then all my debts and more will be fully repaid. Now, is my meal ready?"

The uncle smiled a sly, greedy smile.

The captain nodded.

The uncle sat down at a table laid with dishes of silver. There were puddings and pies and peaches and cream. He began to eat.

"Is it to your liking?" asked the captain.

"Well enough," said Matilda's uncle, one arm still cradling the churn. "But I wish there was a little more salt."

Chinkelly chunk ... chunk... the churn's handle began to turn, slowly at first.

"Stop!" shrieked the uncle, clinging to the handle. "STOP!"

CHUNKELLY CHINK ... CHINKELLY CHUNK ... the handle went faster.

The uncle was very pale. Nothing he did, nothing he said made the handle stop turning. Salt spilled out, more and more and more.

The ship's cabin filled with salt. All the crew swept and tossed the salt overboard as the deck was heaped with salt, but it was no use. The deck was piled high. The salt reached the lowest sails, then the highest – and higher. The ship reeled and heeled, and the ship's crew leapt into a little boat and rowed furiously away across the sea.

The ship heaved and sighed and sank – down to the sands at the very bottom of the ocean. No one ever saw the uncle again, but down in the dark depths of the wide and rolling sea, as blue and as green as a kingfisher's wing, the churn went on turning. Chinkelly chunk, chunkelly chink…

A few days later, Matilda was sitting at the edge of the sea, dabbling her hand in the water. "That's odd," she said, as she licked her fingers. "I do believe the sea tastes different."

"What does it taste of?" asked her littlest sister.

"Well," Matilda said, "it tastes of salt."

And so it did...

And so it does...

And so it always will.